Clifford's
Good Deeds

Norman Bridwell

SCHOLASTIC INC.

For Tim, Steve, and Paul

All rights reserved. Published by Scholastic Inc., *Publishers since 1920.* SCHOLASTIC and associated logos are trademarks and/or registered trademarks of Scholastic Inc.

The publisher does not have any control over and does not assume any responsibility for author or third-party websites or their content.

Library of Congress Cataloguing-in-Publication Data is available.

ISBN: 978-0-545-21579-4

40 39 38 37 36   20 21 22 23

Printed in Jefferson City, MO, USA   40
This edition printing, September 2019

Scholastic Inc., 557 Broadway, New York, NY 10012
Scholastic UK Ltd., Euston House, 24 Eversholt Street, London NW1 1DB

Hello. I'm Emily Elizabeth.

This is my dog, Clifford.

A boy named Tim lives across the street.

One day Tim said, "I try to do
a good deed every day. If I had Clifford
I could help a lot of people."
I said, "Let's do some good deeds together."

A man was raking leaves. Tim gave him a hand.
Then we helped him put the leaves in his truck.

I didn't know that dry leaves . . .

. . . make Clifford sneeze.

AH-CHOO

The man said he didn't need any more help.
We went down the street.

We saw a lady painting her fence.

We helped her paint.
When we finished she thanked us.

Clifford felt so happy that he
wagged his tail. That was a mistake.
White paint splattered all over
her house.

We said we would paint the rest of her house too.
The lady said, "Never mind."

Then we saw an old lady
trying to get her kitten down from a tree.
Tim said, "Clifford, get the kitty."

Clifford bent the limb down
so the lady could reach her kitten.

But his paw slipped.

Clifford moves pretty fast for a big dog.

The lady was glad to get her kitten back.

It didn't take us long to find
our next good deed to do.

Somebody had let the air out of the tires
of a car. The man asked if we could help him.

Tim took a rubber tube out of the car
and stuck it on the tire valve. Then he
told Clifford to blow air through the tube.

Clifford blew.

But he blew a little too hard.

The man felt better when we took his car to a garage.

We saw a small paperboy.
He was so small that he couldn't throw
the newspapers to the doorsteps.

Clifford gave him a hand. I mean a paw.

Clifford was a little too strong.

Nothing seemed to go right for us.

All our good deeds were turning out wrong.

Then we saw a terrible thing. A man was hurt
and lying in the street. Nobody was helping him.

Tim said, "You should never move
an injured person." Clifford didn't hear him.
He picked the man up.

We started off to find a doctor. Oh dear.

We helped the men get their cable
back down the manhole. Tim said, "Clifford,
maybe you shouldn't help me anymore."

Clifford felt very sad. He had tried so hard
to do the right things. We headed for home.

Suddenly we heard somebody shouting,
"Help! Fire!"

The house on the corner was on fire.

Tim ran to the alarm box

to call the fire department.

Clifford ran to the burning house.

There were two little kids upstairs.

With Clifford's help we got them out safely.

Luckily, there was a swimming pool in the yard.

Clifford put out the fire just as the firemen were arriving.

The firemen finished the job
and thanked us for our help.

That afternoon the mayor gave us
each a medal for our good deeds.

Of course, Clifford got the biggest medal of all.